Words From The Heart: Poems For Grandma

Troya Hohlfeld

Words From The Heart: Poems For Grandma
© 2022 Troya Hohlfeld

All rights reserved.

Presentation by *BookLeaf Publishing*

Web: www.bookleafpub.com

E-mail: info@bookleafpub.com

ISBN: 9789357619592

First edition 2022

This book is dedicated to my Grandma Faith Ann. Always on my mind and always in my heart now and forever.

ACKNOWLEDGEMENT

To anyone who has ever lost their grandmother or someone close to your heart who you considered to be your grandmother.

My Heart

My heart is filled with pain
It's as bad as the pouring rain
My heart is filled with sadness
Nothing more and nothing less
My heart is nearly gone
Disappearing with the new dawn
My heart will never be whole again
It's too hard to explain
My heart is filled with pain
It forever has a stain
My heart is filled with sadness
Can't take too much more I guess
My heart is nearly gone
And to my grandma, I will always belong
My heart will never be whole again
Who am I to complain?

How

How can I tell my heart that you have gone
away
When I think about you every day
I am lonely and sad I still can't believe you are
gone
And I see your face in the morning with each
new dawn
But others tell me to get over it that I must move
on
As your picture, I gaze upon
But they don't know how I feel
I am not sure my heart will ever fully heal
One minute I was happy and then my world was
ripped apart
Like a knife right to the heart
Yes I need to mourn and in my own way
And not listen to what others say
There will be dark times
As often as the noon bell chimes
Yes I will be sad
And that is not a reason to be mad
It will hurt for a while
But I will never forget your smile
Time may ease some of the sorrow
As I look toward tomorrow

There will be many tears
As I go through the years
I may scream and shout
But sometimes I just need to pout
I can't lock the pain away
In my heart, you will always stay.

The Day

The day you went away
Hurt me more than I can say
I know it's been 7 years
But I still cry many tears
I miss our heart-to-heart talks
And our weekly walks
I miss seeing you smile when you saw me
When I spent time with you I felt so free
Grandma, I miss you so very much
If only there was a way we could have stayed in
touch
The day you went away
I can see it in my head every day
Life hasn't really moved on for me
I'm being the best person I can be
The day you went away
Was the day my world turned gray.

Send Me Love

You send me love from Heaven
But I know that one day I will see you again
Sending me love is your way of letting me know
that your pain is gone
I feel your presence daily with each new dawn
While your pain is gone mine is not
Now pictures of you are all I have got
Yes I know that you are in a better place
But I wish I could see your smiling face
I try not to cry even though I have lost you
Wishing you were here for everything that I am
going through
You send me love from Heaven
And I think I see glimpses of you every now and
then.

Never

I will never forget my grandmother
To me, she was my mother
I will never forget the fun times we had
She comforted me when I was sad
I will never forget how much she loved me
To my heart, she will always hold the key
I will never forget how much I loved her
Feel like I'm sitting on a permanent burr
I will never forget the look on her face when I
was around
And to my heart, she will always be bound
I will never forget the love that we did share
That kind of love is rare
I will never forget my grandmother
She can be compared to no other.

Hi Grandma

Hi grandma I just wanted to say hi
Since I couldn't say bye
I try not to be sad
But I really miss the grandma I once had
So I'm just here
Trying not to shed a tear
I'm missing you like crazy
Can't see through to the light it's too hazy
I know that you're in a better place
Sitting with the King of Grace
I hope everything is going good
I would visit you if I could
You will always have my love
While you watch from above
Hi grandma I just wanted to say hi
As the day grows nigh.

Christmas In Heaven

As I look around I see many decorated
Christmas trees
And don't forget the cold breeze
The lights on each tree shine bright but they
don't compare to the beauty of Heaven's light
There are not enough words to describe that
beautiful sight
I smile and try not to shed a tear
But I know that you are celebrating Christmas in
Heaven again this year
I have heard and also listened to many different
Christmas songs
Such as Silent Night and Joy To The World
But even the joys of Christmas do not come
close
To the one, I miss the most
I can't even imagine what Christmas in Heaven
would be like
I would come to visit but I don't think I can take
that hike
The angels singing in the Heavenly choir must
sound so amazing
As the angels sing their praises
And while I continue to sing
I know you are walking with the King

So grandma I will say Merry Christmas in
Heaven.

9 Years

It's been a little over 9 years
But that doesn't stop the tears
People say I should have been over it a long
time ago
They just don't understand me though
What people don't understand is that I will never
get over "it" never
I will love you forever
People don't understand that "it" is my precious
irreplaceable grandmother
She was unlike any other
I am not trying to but I am starting to forget the
small things
And that really pulls on my heartstrings
Things like the sound of her voice
But one day I will join her in Heaven and we
will both rejoice
I feel like if I would have done more you would
still be here with me
And my heart would be pain-free
It's been a little over 9 years
I'm hoping to see your face when the sky clears.

I Miss You

I miss you more than words can say
With each passing day
I can't believe that you're gone
Without you, the days are so long
I miss you more than anyone knows
Now my mood has so many lows
I wish I could see you just once more
But you're beyond Heaven's Door
I miss you more than people think
Sometimes I see your face when I blink
I hope you're doing good up there
You better play fair
I miss you more than all the love everywhere
And for you, I will always care
I will never forget you
And I love you for everything you used to do
I miss you more than words can say
As I watch the sunrise over the bay.

Let You Go

I know I should let you go
But I don't really know how to do so
It's been over three years I should try and move
on
To your picture, I will always be drawn
Grandma, I don't know if I'm ready
Your face I wish I could see
Is it wrong to still miss you so much
I wish we could keep in touch
As I write this I try not to cry
Instead, I just sigh
I love you grandma so I will let you go
Now my mood is very low.

Forever

I haven't heard your voice in years
Which is enough to bring on the tears
My heart still has conversations with you every
day
I wish I could see you if only there was a way
There is nothing or no one who can replace a
loved one who is gone
Don't ever let anyone tell you when to move on
Losing a loved one leaves an emptiness that
doesn't go away
In my heart, you will forever stay.

Without You At Christmas

Do you know how much you are missed
Seeing you again is at the top of my Christmas
list
You are watching over me so you already know
I am trying to get through this before my tears
flow
But I know that you are with me wherever I go
I still wish I could see you though
It doesn't take much for me to be reminded of
you
Do you remember everything that we used to do
Being here without you at Christmas is still not
right
But I still think of you each day when the day
turns to night.

A Reason

People say there is a reason
That things will get better with the change of the
season
People think that time will heal
But they have no idea how I feel
Neither of these will ever take away the pain
And no one can hear you if you cry in the rain
I think it's funny how people think you can get
over a loved one's death so easily
Can't say that I agree even though my grandma
is watching over me peacefully
No one will ever know the amount of pain I hold
in my heart
I couldn't even tell you where to start
I can't even tell you how many times I have
broken down and cried
But most of the pain I feel I hide
There is so much I wish I could tell you
But you are beyond my view.

Don't

Don't forget about me while you're up there
The pain I feel without you is hard to bear
Don't forget about the love I have for you
I miss everything we used to do
Don't forget about the times
Even if we only had a couple of dimes
Don't forget about everything we shared
And I know that for me you always cared
Don't forget about how much I care
People like you are very rare
Don't forget about how much you meant to me
To your heart, I hold the key
Don't forget about me grandmother
There will never be another.

Grandma

Dear grandma, you were and are my best friend
Any problem I had you could mend
It's been three years and I still miss you so much
I long for just one touch
I am trying to hold onto the memories
As I look out to the seas
I hope you are watching over me
And I am trying to be all that I can be
I love you and miss you grandmother
You were unlike any other.

Heaven

As you sit in Heaven
I try not to cry again
You watch over me every day
And you hear everything that I say
I try to watch for signs
Every morning when the sun shines
I wish you had never gone away
But I know you couldn't stay
You hear me when I'm laughing
Not knowing what the day will bring
And you watch me when I sleep
When I dream of you I often weep
You often place your arms around me
In those moments I feel so free
I need your comfort when I weep
The pain of missing you goes so deep
Wish I could go back in time
But every day you help me climb
I want to have you here with me
But I know that can never be
Sometimes I can't help but feel alone
Like I am on my own
I feel bad that I am here and you are not
But since you are up in Heaven save me a spot

Heaven must be truly beautiful since they have
you
I shall miss you and love you forever too
Life goes on this I know
It just isn't the same though
I think of you with every breath that I take
Don't think I can handle any more heartbreak.

Words

Words can't describe how much I miss my
grandmother
For there was no one like her
I was there when she died
And oh how I cried
I think about her all the time
Half the time I cry on a rhyme
Words can't describe how much she meant to me
My love for her is deeper than the sea
I think about her every day
She always knew what to say
I feel so lost without her
Like a bear without his fur
Words will never take away the pain I feel
It will take a while for me to heal.

My Grandma

My grandma was the greatest person I ever
knew
She was always there no matter what I was
going through
One thing I loved about her is that whenever she
saw me she would always smile
Then we would sit and talk for a while
I love the way she spoke her mind
But she always knew when to be kind
Now she's in a better place
I just wish I could see her face
It hasn't been the same without her here
Because I no longer have her listening ear
I know that you are in Heaven as happy as can
be
Just hoping that you are watching over me
Keep your grandma close to you and visit her as
much as you can
Because you don't know God's plan.

Your Birthday

It's almost your birthday
There is so much I want to say
Grandma, I wish you were here so together we
could celebrate
And have some cake on a plate
You filled my life with love
Now you're watching over me from above
But it just isn't the same
I hope this doesn't sound lame
I miss our talks
And our weekly walks
As I soon celebrate your birthday
I send much love your way.

Memories

I have so many memories of us
I remember when you used to put me on the bus
There was the time we went to the movies
And saw the hottie of the seven seas
But my memories aren't enough
It's getting so hard to stay tough
No words can describe how much I miss you
I don't know what to do
Without you, I am so lost
To have you back I would pay any cost.

You Taught Me

You taught me how to walk
And how to talk
You taught me how to tie my shoe
And how to say moo
You taught me how to read
And how to do a good deed
You taught me how to share
And how to care
You taught me how to cook
And how to read a book
You taught me how to love
And about Jesus up above.

www.ingramcontent.com/pod-product-compliance
Lightning Source LLC
La Vergne TN
LVHW021355200726
843509LV00014B/2856